Hélène Druvert

New York Melody

Thames & Hudson

Hush, everyone! Let the concert now start.
The musicians are ready to each play their part.

For Marin — This story was written for you, one night when you wouldn't sleep.
For Manu and Seb, who cleverly turned three little notes into a tune.
Hélène

Translated from the French *New York Melody*

First published in the United Kingdom in 2018 by
Thames & Hudson Ltd, 181A High Holborn,
London WC1V 7QX

www.thamesandhudson.com

First published in the United States of America in 2018 by
Thames & Hudson Inc., 500 Fifth Avenue, New York, New York 10110

www.thamesandhudsonusa.com

Original edition © 2017 Gautier-Languereau / Hachette Livre, Paris
This edition © 2018 Thames & Hudson Ltd, London

British Library Cataloguing-in-Publication Data
A catalogue record for this book is available from the British Library.

Library of Congress Control Number 2018932495

ISBN   978-0-500-65173-5

Printed and bound in China

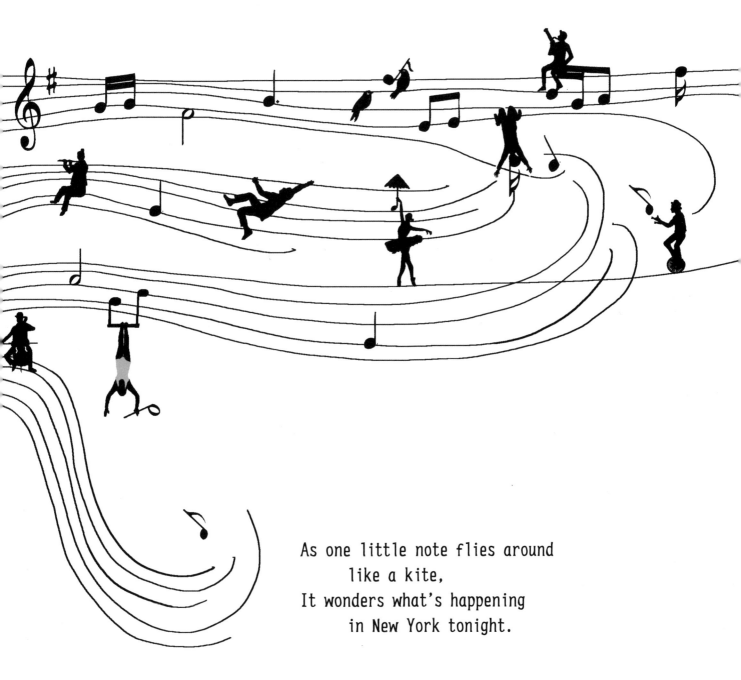

As one little note flies around
like a kite,
It wonders what's happening
in New York tonight.

So secretly,
    while the piano keys play,

        In search of adventure,
            it flutters away.

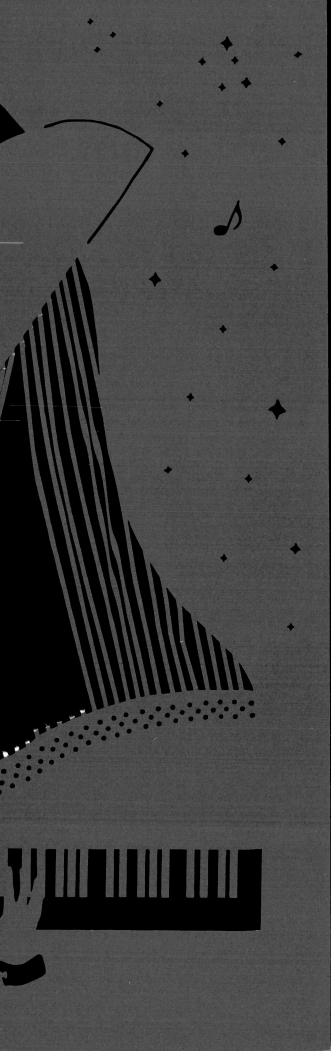

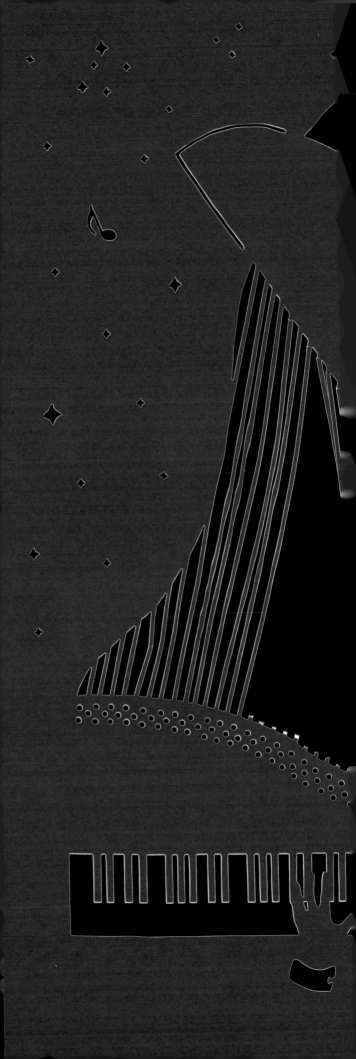

Carnegie Hall is soon left far behind,
As the note disappears to see what it can find...

Broadway is twinkling
   with bright lights galore.
The note spots a jazz club
   and sneaks through the door.